Echoes at the Fountain

Jim McKeon

First Published 1999

© Copyright Jim McKeon 1999

Published by
ACORN PRESS CORK
Paddock House
Sunvalley Drive
Cork
Tel: 021-393347
email jamesmckeon@hotmail.com

ISBN 0 9528248 1 7

Printed in Ireland by Litho Press Co., Midleton, Co. Cork.

To my parents
Eileen and Jim
They gave me life
They gave me love

In many ways this book wrote itself. I had been writing a weekly column for the Evening Echo and hardly a day went by without someone asking me to put the columns together in book form. This is the end product. It is 25 nostalgic chapters on events, places and people who have touched, influenced and improved my life. I wish to thank the kindness of the Examiner; the Evening Echo, especially the editor, Brian Feeney; Justin Nelson of the Clonmel Nationalist; Wolfehound Press; the Barry family; and all those patient, charming and wonderful librarians of Cork; but most of all I'd like to thank the people I wrote about. They took me into their hearts and into their homes. This book is for them. Below is an extract from a poem I wrote many years ago when I was fourteen. The poem was about an old man, on his eighty-first birthday, sitting alone by his fire and thinking back on his own childhood. Since I wrote that simple poem the clock of life has moved on and now, almost into the year 2000, it has much more relevance.

'I recall adventures of my youth
each filled with joy and pleasure
The pranks I played, each orchard raid
is now a heart-kept treasure
We were always full of fun
and looking for a laugh
like the times we played cowboys
on farmer Reilly's calf
In the club we had when we were young
We passed the time away
The rafters rung with the songs we sung
They echo still today '

Jim McKeon Oct 1999

Contents

Christmas Memories

The Christmases of my childhood meant many things: the joy of school holidays, the innocent excitement at Santa's arrival, presents, the cinema, visiting cribs, the panto, and snow. It always seemed to be snowing which shows how selective the memory can be. But, for me, it wasn't all fun. We lived in a grey farmhouse at the top of a long, winding lane and we kept chickens, geese, goats, pigs and a donkey. Now pigs have to be fed even on school holidays. Every day I had to tackle up the donkey and cart, call to every house in the neighbourhood, and collect the leftover food from their dinners. Although there was a certain standing as, chariot-like, I went about my business, in effect, I hated this daily, time-consuming chore while my pals played football.

We knew Christmas had arrived when the tree appeared in the the front room. This was my father's job and he always made me feel special by asking me to help him. It was nothing elaborate or flashy; just a plane tree he had chopped down, stuck in a bucket of sand and plonked in the corner but, to me, it was magical. Then the big, red candle was

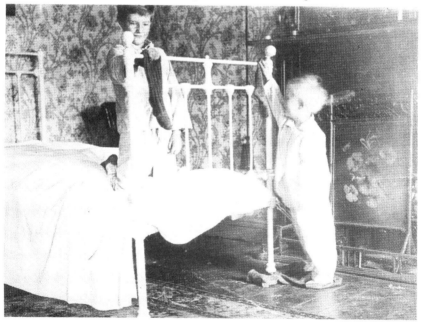

Hanging up the stocking.
COURTESY EXAMINER

1

symbolically placed in the window and lit by the youngest in the family. Christmas was on its way.

My mother usually went to the cinema on Sunday night while my father "looked after us." If any of us cried he just picked us up, put us out in the yard, and locked the door until we stopped. It worked every time. Another night she returned to find my eldest brother playing INSIDE the fireguard. My father explained sheepishly that, at least, he knew where the child was. He gave me six pence every week. The cinema was three pence; westerns were enjoyed with an animated passion and we rode imaginary horses, shooting imaginary indians, all the way home. Then, it was a bag of chips for tuppence and, finally, six rock-like toffees for the last penny. My father was an extremely kind and sometimes frustrating man. One Christmas I saved up and bought him a heavy, woollen jumper. A few days later a local man, who was a little down in his luck, passed our house. I couldn't help but notice that he was wearing my present. Like all youngsters, I thought my father would live forever and when he died suddenly I cried for months.

Usually about a week before Christmas, the last day at school before the holidays was extra special. Lessons were forgotten as the whole school was assembled to sing Christmas carols. We always finished up with a rousing rendition of "Silent Night."

The excitement on Christmas morning was almost unbearable. Sleep was impossible. We woke at dawn and, anxious not to wake our parents, we quietly checked our stockings. Then it was early mass and communion, and after breakfast we all met at the bottom of the lane to compare presents. Looking back, they were fairly mundane: a toy gun or holster, simple games like ludo or snakes and ladders, a rubber football, a comic annual or a cap-gun which was great until the caps ran out. Similarly, the girls got presents like colouring books, plastic tea sets or dolls. This particular Christmas I was delighted with a beautiful silver flashlamp. To my utter disappointment it had no batteries. One boy, an only child who lived half a mile away, once received a bicycle. We were green with envy but he allowed us to ride up and down the lane at a penny a time.

The highlight of the day was the Christmas dinner. It was always stuffed goose followed by potatoes in their jackets cooked over the open fire, and roast apples dipped in brown sugar. It seemed to go on forever. This was all washed down with cool, diluted rasberry. As the day wore on there was a never-ending stream of visitors: friends, neighbours, aunts, uncles and distant cousins. Few left before sampling the Christmas spirit. Others lingered on and weren't slow in giving a blast of a song or two.

St Stephen's day was another early start. Half a dozen of us wren boys met at an agreed spot and sang our way up one side of the lane and down the other. That was our patch. It was an unwritten rule. We never ventured further afield. Most houses gave us a few pence, probably to get rid of us. We disappeared to carefully count our loot. This was very important because the size of the amount decided whether we went to the local film or to one of the posher cinemas in town. If the takings were really good we might even afford the luxury of ice cream or sweets on our way home.

After St Stephen's day the excitement petered out. We spent our time lying on in bed reading comics and listening to the radio, visiting other churches and comparing the different cribs, or we kept busy by building a big snowman in the quarry behind the lane. Our pleasures were simple. How times have changed.

Snowball fight – note barefoot boy on left.
COURTESY EXAMINER

3

Doing Pana

I was asked recently what Patrick St meant to me. The question set me thinking. A thousand memories flashed across my mind. In most cities the main thoroughfare is usually straight but, like a giant meandering snake, Patrick St twists and turns from Patrick's Bridge to the Grand Parade. Also, the city centre is relatively small and has the warm intimacy of a village. Take my hand and walk with me along the Patrick St of my youth.

Let us start at number one - the Gas Company showrooms. Next is Melina's beauty salon. Melina's has special memories for me because in my wayward, teenage years I walked out with a pretty girl who worked there, but that's a story for another day. Next stop is that beautiful, old-world shop, Mangan's, the watchmakers and opticians. On the footpath opposite their front door stands the famous old clock which has been the meeting place for countless courting couples down through the years. Next door is the Tivoli Restaurant which has a certain fame because when the King and Queen of England visited Cork in 1903 this was where the royal couple had lunch. Moving on quickly there is Santry's snuff and tobacco shop, Leupold the photographer, Blair's chemist, Halo hairdressers, the Soveriegn Bar, Andrews newsagents, O'Shea tailors, Bacon Shops Ltd, Simcox grocery and Tyler's shoe shop on the corner. Then there is the booksellers, Educational Company of Ireland.

Nowadays, it is a common sight to see a plethora of waiting taxis in the rank opposite where this shop was. Some years back taxis were few and far between - only a handful in this rank - and if a car was needed, the customer was obliged to ring the phone which hung precariously on a solitary poll.

Patrick St now begins to turn as we approach two of the city's finest shops: Roches Stores and Cashs. While passing this area my mind dwells on that awful night of madness in December 1920 when British forces burned down a large section of the city. These two shops were the first to be attacked. Thankfully, those traumatic days are long gone.

Returning to our stroll, right on the bend, at the corner of Winthrop St, is the Lee Cinema. This intimate venue holds many memories for me. Once, a friend and I had agreed to go to the Lee with two girls on a warm Sunday night. At the last minute my friend changed his mind and went to the pub on his own. I ended up in the front row, an unmerciful crick in my neck, flanked by two girls. I'll never forget that film: Sands across the

Desert. While my tongue was hanging out with the thirst, my friend was drinking pints of Guinness in the Long Valley. It took me years to forgive him.

Across from the Lee is Cudmore's shop(recently gone), Commercial College, Fitzgerald's tailors, Cork Art Club, O'Regan hosiers, Miss Todd hairdresser, and McKechnies dyers near the corner of the long, dull Robert St. I recall Robert St with mixed feelings. I was a young telegram boy working in the nearby GPO, and we had access to occasional tips in the telegrams from England. There was a betting office at the end of Robert St which was strictly out of bounds but we often put our last shilling on Fred Winter or Lester Piggot. As our bosses, who also got these tips, frequented this office we were sometimes caught red-handed.

At the corner we come to another old-world shop - the Munster Arcade. Next to the Arcade is Egan's jewellers. When I was a twelve-year-old schoolboy I was farmed out to Egan's for a while. It was my first job. One of my many duties was to open the back door which was situated in Elbow Lane, off Cook St, and prepare the shop for the 9am opening. I

Patrick Street – What traffic?
COURTESY EXAMINER

5

seemed to spend all my time polishing glass and brass in the ecclesiastical department; at the time, the word ecclesiastical was bigger than myself. I didn't know what it meant but I used to drop it casually into conversation with my friends. They were very impressed. After a few weeks in Egan's I was given a man's long dustcoat which touched my ankles. One day my boss took me aside and said, "Your coat is too short". Unaware of his sarcasm, I replied innocently, "No, sir. It's too long". Shortly afterwards I was returned to school. Around that time I had the enormous responsibility of ringing the angelus bell in the North Cathedral at six o'clock every day. In my naive innocence I thought that this was the only angelus bell in Cork.

Going on from Egan's we have the Economy Shop, another Tyler's shoe shop, the graceful Victoria Hotel, Aer Lingus, Irish Independent office, to the end of the block and THE shop in Cork - Woolworth's. Woolworth's was a child's heaven; you could get everything there: toys, ice cream, a variety of sweets and delicious broken chocolate. Let us move reluctantly on to the Fifty Shilling Tailors, Saxone Shoes, Cake Room, Miss Murphy hairdresser, Polyfoto Ltd, Blackthorn House, Cavendish's, and Burton's on the corner where you got the suit for that special occasion. After Burton's there is the Man's Shop, Grant's, and McTighe's tobacconists as we pass Market Lane, the Oyster and Market Bars, BMC Stores and the famous Dan Hobbs' shop; Dan was one of Cork's great characters. We are almost at the halfway mark with four clothes shops in a row: Tom Murphy's, Mannix and Culhane's, Buckley's and Con Murphy's. Then, right up to the final bend, it's Roche's jewellers, Barry's tobacconist and, finally, at the corner of the Grand Parade, O'Callaghan's chemist. Let us cross over and do the other side of Pana.

At the corner of Daunt's Sq is Woodford Bourne's. I want to linger here for a brief moment and close my eyes and take in that unique smell of groceries, wine and tea. Next door is Fielding's chemist followed by the Provincial Bank, McCarthy and Kearney tailors, and Archer's jewellers which seemed to be up ten flights of stairs. If memory serves me right we then had Fitzsimon's shop, Guy's printers, Thompson's confectionary, Lipton's, Nathan's tailors, Bolger's stores, Miss Lucey hairdresser, Gerald Barry's ladies outfitters and Elvery's sports shop which had a replica of an elephant over the front door. As young boys, we got all our sports gear here. I distinctly remember that the hurleys cost a staggering one and sixpence (7½p). Next to Elvery's is P J Mockler's fur shop, and right on the bend is the Pavillion Cinema with its beautiful,

A bustling Patrick Street 70 years ago.
COURTESY EXAMINER

7

white marble front. This was more than just a cinema; it was a great meeting and eating place in the poshest of surroundings. Whenever there was a special date, when trying to impress a girl, it was always the Pav, tea and cream cakes, and then the film. Now heading for Patrick's Bridge, we pass J J Barry's, Brennan's jewellers, Hipp's tailors, Brown Thompson seedmen, Murray's gunsmiths, the Ulster Bank, the Moderne shop and MacSweeny's chemist at the corner of Academy St. On the far corner is Barter's tourist office, the Green Door restaurant, Le Chateau Bar, London and Newcastle Tea Company, the Examiner office, O'Flynn's butchers, John's shop, British Rail, Smith's Stores, Miss Cummins' chiropody, Mayne's Chemist, the Methodist church, the Leprechaun restaurant, Foley's beautiful sweet shop, Clancy's wine shop and then Robert Day's harnessmakers. Again, the smell of the leather and polish comes back to me. Then we had Joseph Mayne's china shop and Dunnes Stores before we cross the narrow lane to Lester's chemist and the Savoy Cinema. The Savoy has been the Mecca for generations of Corkonians down through the years, especially before the arrival of television. It was practically impossible to gain admission to this magical venue on Sunday night. You had to have a season ticket and I can well remember the lengthy queues. Tickets were like gold dust; you couldn't get one even on the black market. The atmosphere was electric on Monday nights. Always packed, not alone did you see a film, but the audience also had a singsong. They were accompanied by organist, Fred Bridgeman, as the words of the songs appeared on the screen. At this time I worked as a young postman delivering letters to the Savoy and Pavillion cinemas. One of the perks of this duty was that I got two complimentary tickets for both cinemas every week. The Savoy was also used for cabaret and some of the visiting stars that spring to mind are Harry Secombe, Val Doonican and Tom Jones.

Leaving the Savoy we come to Tailorfit's, the Cork Hardware Company, the Steampacket Company, Dowden's costume makers, Pigott's record shop, Kingston's shoes, Vard's furs, Gilbert's, Dooley's estate agents, Barry and Hyland's shoe shop, the Old Bridge Restaurant and, finally, that great sporting bar, the Swan and Cygnet.

Our brief stroll down memory lane has come to an end. As we stand on the corner, I can look off to my left and follow the vast skyline of the northside. Away up to the right are the distant mansions of Montenotte, and right in front of me is Shandon Steeple with its four faces glowering down at the people in Patrick St.

Where Are They Now?

One of the sadder aspects of modern life is the almost complete disappearance of our "characters". When I was a wee lad growing up in the city there seemed to be an abundance of them. Their names still haunt me: Holy Joe, Burn the Water, Rashers, Dinny Drake, Slobby Malone, Andy Gaw, The Melodian Man, Rosie, Molly the Dogs, Cidona Willy, The Rancher, Klondyke, The Galloping Major, Dicky Glue, Forty Coats, Born Drunk, Duck the Bullet and Dr Any-Dogs. And I'm sure there are many more. Each had his own idyosyncrasy, his own personal trademark. For

instance, Dr Any-Dogs dreaded dogs, and whenever he went to the house of a sick child he would knock on the door, then run across the street and call out to the woman of the house, "Mrs, any dogs?" If the answer was "no" he would go in and see the child. But if there was a dog in the house the woman would have to hold the child out the window so that the doctor could examine it. Rosie was a small, innocuous, little man who wore a cap, and always had a rose in his lapel. He could be seen all over town blowing kisses to all and sundry. The Rancher used to sell blocks of timber and bundles of sticks from a box car. When he got bored, he turned the car upside down, stood on it and gushed his war cry: 'Burn the Rancher's blocks and you'll have hell on earth.'

In recent years these colourful "characters" are conspicuous by their absence. Like old soldiers they simply faded away.

This colourul character is holding his own.
COURTESY EXAMINER

9

My own favourite, in the sixties, was Donie (flick the penny) Murphy. He had a magnetic appeal to us and was like the pied piper of Hamlin as we followed him everywhere. Donie had the amazing ability to throw a penny over his shoulder, back-heel it fifteen feet up in the air and then miraculously catch the spinning coin in his top pocket. He never missed. It must have taken years of practice. In the summer months our American visitors loved him. Unfortunately, decimalization ruined Donie's career. Like many of us, he never really adjusted to the new currency. I remember once, a foreign television crew filmed him in action. The fee was paid in porter.

Furthermore, being an avid reader of the death column in the Evening Echo and a great man for funerals, or should I say in the pub after funerals, he managed to materialise on the outer fringes of the mourners. The man was an artist to his fingertips. He had a line of patter down to a fine art and, with perfect timing, the first move was "will you have a Woodbine, boy?" (it never ceases to amaze me how everyone in Cork remains a boy). Donie's Woodbine was a sort of sprat. Of course, naturally, reciprocation would raise its beautiful head and, with a pint is

his hand and his foot in the door, as it were, Donie would display his vast repertoire: " ah, sure, the poor child, she's in heaven" or "errah, he had a long life and he went grand and quick." From five to ninety-five Donie always had the appropriate song or verse in Irish, English or Latin. You always got value for your pint. He was definitely a man for all seasons; few people were aware that he was once a Brother in Mount Melleray and, also, that he was an accomplished pianist.

Sadly, I haven't seen him for years, although I did hear that he occasionally makes guest appearances at important funerals. He is a dying breed. May he live forever.

Popular accordian player
on Patricks Bridge.
COURTESY BARRY FAMILY

Billa O'Connell
Prince of Panto

Billa O'Connell was born on Christmas day 1929. The youngest of six children, he was christened William Christopher and was reared near the Lough. "Although I played with Lough Rovers, like my father before me I'm a true-blue Barr's man all my life." For as far back as he can remember he has been involved in pantomime one way or another. Panto has always played a big part in the O'Connell household at Christmas. In his early school days in Sullivans Quay he has vivid memories of his brother and two sisters performing in pantos, and as a young boy he sold programmes in Fr O'Leary Hall. Then he took to the boards and appeared in several school concerts. "David McInerney was an old school pal. He was a lovely violinist and I used to do a lot of singing then. In recent years, any time he bumps into me in town, he loves to remind me of our happy days in Sullivans Quay."

Dame Billa

The old Opera House was the centre of Cork theatre then. It had an old-world atmosphere all of its own. That was in the days before television. You could count yourself lucky to get in. It was always packed. The stars were Jimmie O'Dea, Maureen Potter, Jack Cruise and, of course, Ignatius Comerford. He had everything.

Billa was just 18 when he made his debut as the dame in Cinderella at the Fr O'Leary Hall. Paddy Coughlan and Paddy Cotter, two future stars of the Swans, were the ugly sisters. He was immediately hooked. The following year he was asked to play the dame in Babes in the Wood at the AOH Hall. He jumped at the chance. He was now the dame at the AOH

11

Hall and the inimitable Ignatius Comerford was the dame at the Opera House. At that time a show called Up Cork was staged every spring in AOH Hall. Unfortunately, Ignatius became ill and Billa was asked to take over as the dame in the Up Corks. The show made theatrical history and broke all records. It ran for 16 weeks at the AOH Hall and when it finished it toured Counties Cork and Kerry for several weeks. With no opposition, live shows were very popular then, and Billa was now so busy that he was booked up most weekends from October to April.

Then tragedy struck. "We were rehearsing Sleeping Beauty in the Old Opera House two weeks before Christmas 1955. Jim Stack was directing and we were using the upstairs bar. There was a smell of smoke and we could hear a crackling noise. We thought it was the dancers rehearsing down on the stage. Anyway, the fire brigade arrived. Paddy Cotter asked Stack if the rehearsal was over. He replied, 'No. We'll resume when the fire brigade are gone.' When we came out the roof was blazing." It was to take 10 long years before the new Opera House was built. Sleeping Beauty was brought to the AOH Hall but that building caught fire and the panto never went on. For years nobody would touch Sleeping Beauty. They thought there was a jinx on it.

Then Billa's career took another twist when he was offered a straight acting part in John Power's great play, As Some Tall Cliff, directed by Jim Stack. The cast included Michael McAuliffe, Lorraine Jones, Bill O'Mahoney, Rex Archer and Paddy Cotter, and it was a huge success.

Summer Revels arrived in the early seventies. It was a highly popular show sprinkled with local humour, political satire, dancing and good music. The top-class cast included Paddy Comerford, Cha and Miah, the Montfords, McTaggert dancers, Barrett and Sullivan, David McInerney and Marie Twomey. Summer Revels ran for 21 incredible years, once packing the Opera House for six weeks.

Billa has had many memorable moments in his career and also feels very lucky to have had 30 fabulous years working in Beamish's Brewery. He has appeared with some great performers; there are some lovely memories and he's still friends with them all. There were several appearances on the Late Late Show including the All Cork night. That was special. Even today, people are constantly looking for a tape of it. He was at a match one night and this priest approached him. "Are you Billa?" he asked. "I am, Father," was the reply. "I saw you in Africa," the priest said. "I'm not known outside Mitchelstown," said Billa. "No. You don't understand," the priest laughed. "I saw you in Africa on the All Cork Late Late Show."

Of all the venues he played, The Wembley Conference Centre stands out. It holds 3,500 people. He was given the number two dressingroom and there was a star on the door with his name on it. Billa was thrilled with this. "God forgive me," he recalls. "But one night when no one was looking I stuffed the star up my jumper and took it home with me. I still have it."

Billa O'Connell has had a long and happy life. "I think the man above kept an eye on me. I have 16 lively grandchildren to keep me busy but, most of all, there's my wife, Nell. We're married nearly 44 years. She's not just my wife; she's my best pal, too. I'd be lost without her. We go for long walks together and I swim every day."

In 1996 UCC bestowed on him an honorary MA degree and 1998 was a year he'll never forget. To mark his fiftieth year in panto the Lord Mayor presented him with a beautiful silver tray at a civic reception in the City Hall. He accepted it with genuine humility. "This is not just for me." he said. "But for all the wonderful people I've worked with who made it possible."

Cork Opera House – destroyed 12 December 1955.
COURTESY EXAMINER

13

Pigeon Men

Back in the thirties, old Nicholas Crean, a well-known pigeon man and First World War veteran, was sunning himself in his back yard on Munster Final day. Suddenly, the heavens opened followed by thunder and lightning. A passing pigeon took refuge in his loft. On inspecting the strange bird, he discovered a piece of paper with the result of the match on it. But, more important, also secured to the pigeon's leg was a £5 note. That £5 note was enjoyed by Nicholas and his friends for a week. He never found the destination of the bird. I don't think he tried very hard. Pigeon men will understand.

The first known pigeon club in Cork was in the 1870's - Cork Gentlemen's Flying Club. It was very upper-class then; one had to be vetted before before being allowed to join.

But pigeon racing can be traced way back to Noah's Ark. And it's a fact that Julius Caeser was very fond of pigeons. He regularly sent love notes to Calpurnia in the Coliseum (that was in Rome, now - not MacCurtain St). Other well-known pigeon fanciers were: Queen Elisabeth II and her family. They have lofts in Sandringham. Then, there are Gordon Richards, Roy Rogers, Yul Brynner, Telly Savalas, and soccer men, Gerry Francis and Duncan Ferguson.

The lofts of the famous Jim Biss of Norwich,
arguably the best fancier in the world.

14

Some families in Cork are involved in pigeons all their lives: Peter and Billy Cunneen, Ned and John Power, Ed and Dominick Finnegan, the Crean family, Florrie O'Keeffe, Danny Kenneally, and Tolol Daly who had the famous bird, "Nyjinsky".

There is a long list of unbelievable performances. Thurso, in Northern Scotland (502 miles) is the Grand National of Pigeon racing. But, in the sixties, though he didn't win the race, the late Bill Moynihan had the unique distinction of getting three birds home together. Then Georgie Busteed won Thurso in 1975 and Frazerburg (474 miles) in 1955. Danny Kenneally won Lerwich (633 miles) in 1961. John O'Hare (with help from his brother and father) also won Lerwich in 1978 with a blue hen, and the following week was second out of Thurso with another blue hen. Mick Crean had a great bird: in 1978 he won Perth (376 miles) and two weeks later won the dreaded Thurso - nearly 900 miles in a fortnight.

The golden age of pigeon racing was immediately after both world wars. Hawks, the pigeons' mortal enemy, were eliminated because pigeons delivering important messages were vital in saving lives. Several birds were awarded the Dickens Medal for bravery. This is the equivalent of the Victoria Cross for soldiers. Their is a special museum in Blackpool, England, to commemorate the heroics of pigeons during the war.

Nowadays, hawks are a major problem worldwide. They are being privately bred in conservatories and then let go. Not alone do they attack pigeons but they also kill larks, blackbirds and finches. Recently, at a show in Blackpool, 7,000 pigeon rings were put on display; they had been found in falcons' nests. Many pigeon men recognised their own rings from pigeons which had been missing. To highlight the hawk problem, Mick Crean's bird was the last to fly Thurso on the day. That was in 1981. It hasn't been flown since.

Although pigeon racing isn't as strong as it once was, Cork has always had its colourful characters. One such man was the well-known publican, Johnny O'Mahony. The most important thing in racing is time. Races are often won or lost by seconds. Johnny had his loft up on the roof so that he could clock in his birds quicker. One day he knew that one of his pigeons had done a great time but in his excitement he forgot where he was and fell off the roof. He was the proud owner of a big army motorbike which was as old as himself and, one Sunday after a pigeon convention in Waterford, he offered a friend a ride home to Cork. They had agreed to stop for refreshments on the way back but Johnny flew through each town at unusually high speed with his passenger holding on for dear life. Eventually, they came to a halt at the top of Roman St, and Johnny confessed to his shellshocked friend, "The brakes went halfway up and if I told you you'd have probably jumped off at Youghal."

Another pigeon man's fame had spread cross-channel and Englishmen often travelled over to Cork to buy a bird. The chosen pigeon was always placed in a special brown carrier bag, and wet sawdust was always kindly placed at the bottom of the bag for the pigeon's comfort. As the boat sailed out of Cork Harbour the wet bottom of the bag gave way from the bird's clays and, naturally, like any good bird, it immediately flew back to its loft for a well-deserved feed of fresh corn.

How do pigeons make their way home from hundreds of miles? No one knows. It has been said that they get a bearing from the sun. But there is a growing concern that this modern world of mobile phones, microwaves and satellites creates magnetic fields which complicate the pigeon's orientation.

Billy Cunneen has been involved in pigeons all his life. He went to his eternal reward recently and, at his funeral, in a moving gesture, some pigeons were released. The birds circled the grave in silence for a moment and then in a flash they disappeared as one into the clouds like a soul on its way to heaven. Pigeons are a glorious uncertainty.

Superbird 'Josie Boy' who flew the four longest races back to back – Larne, Mauchline, Perth and Thurso, winning two and placed in two.

Donal Leahy
Celtic Warrior

Donal Leahy was one of the finest centre-forwards ever to don the green shirt of Ireland. Yet he played in every position on the field with Cork Celtic including in goal against Sligo. He was born and reared in Glen Rovers country; his brother, Denis won two county medals with the club and his Uncle Jack was a selector. His first success was with the Blackpool school hurling team. Some of his team-mates were: Bill Carroll, John Kelleher, Pat O'Neill, Dinnie Pa Foley, and T P O'Mahoney who went on to greater things. "We seemed to be forever playing football and hurling," he remembers. "Up in the Green Gardens in Spring Lane by day and in Corcoran's Quay all night." He played with Dunbar Celtic under 14 but when he joined North End minors his career really took off. They won nearly everything that year losing only one match. By now the scouts were beginning to notice this tall, strapping forward who had bags of energy, two good feet and was deadly in the air. He was picked for the Munster youths against West Germany. They won 2-0 at the Mardyke.

1964 Cup Final
COURTESY EXAMINER

17

But it was in the away game in Germany where he scored what was probably his best ever goal. "A cross came in from the wing," he recalled. "I was standing near the edge of the box and I caught it just right with my head. It flew into the roof of the net." He was still minor when he joined Evergreen United in 1956. That team was full of household names: Derry Barrett, Mick O'Keeffe, Con McCarthy, Paul O'Donovan, Séamus Madden and a young Jackie Morley. He was signed to take over from the legendary Big Séanie Mac. Donal scored three goals in his first two games and quickly developed an almost telepathic understanding with Austin Noonan. They were a deadly duo and, for years, they regularly scored over forty goals a season between them. One year, in all competitions, they notched up a staggering total of 76 goals between them. More honours followed. At 18 years of age he represented the League of Ireland against the North on St Patrick's Day. Munster were playing in the hurling Railway Cup on the same day and, as he was getting on the train at Kingsbridge Station, Christy Ring spotted him and came over to enquire about the game. "Christy was my idol. I used to go up to the Glen Field and watch him training and retrieve the sliothars for him. 'How did you get on, Donie?,' he asked me. When I told that we won he was delighted, and when he found out that I had scored Ringy slapped me on the back so hard he nearly broke my shoulder."

Donal went on to represent the National League 17 times. His seven goals scored is still a record and he is the third highest league scorer of all time. In one season Celtic scored over a hundred goals yet lost the league in a play-off. He played against some of the all-time greats: Johnny Haynes, Jack and Bobby Charlton, Bill Brown, Ian Gilzean, John White, Eric Caldow, Pat Crerand, Dave McKay and Jimmy Greaves. He chooses Glasgow Celtic's Bobby Evans as the classiest player he has ever played against.

"The standard of League of Ireland football was very high then. There was Al Finucane, the Hales and Fitzgeralds of Waterford, Freddie Strahan and Eric Barber, Donie Wallace, and, of course, Shamrock Rovers had the likes of Paddy Coad, Liam Tuohy, Paddy Ambrose, Noel Peyton, Johnny Fulham and Ronnie Nolan. Rovers beat us in two cup finals, both after replays, and we could easily have won both, especially in 69."

By then he was carrying a bad back injury. In 1970 Limerick signed him but at the end of that season, after 14 years at the top, he reluctantly hung up his boots. When forced to name his toughest opponent he smiled ruefully and said, "It has to be Pat Davy of Dundalk. By God, he was one hard man."

Donal thinks that the game has changed dramatically in the the last 30 years. "It's all so serious now. The fun is gone out of the game. The characters are all gone. There used to be more attacking play, more goals. Many games spring to mind. We beat St Pat's in one game 8-3. I got five. Another day, away to Sligo, we were winning 9-2 when the game was abandoned with 15 minutes to go. I got three goals the same day. When I turned up for training on the following Tuesday night our manager, Tommy Moroney, called me into his office. He told me that I should have scored three more goals and fined me a week's wages for taking it easy. A few weeks later we were playing in Tolka Park. Shelbourne had just won a European cup match and, before the game, we formed a tunnel and applauded them as they ran on to the pitch. They scored first but we destroyed them 5-2. Afterwards in the dressingroom Ben Hannigan quipped, 'Ye clapped us on to the pitch and then ye kicked us off it.'"

In another match Celtic were away to this well-known League of Ireland team. They were losing 3-1 when the opposing centre-half got an attack of diarrhoea and made a dash for the loo. A few moments later he ran back on to the pitch and said to Donal, "What was all the cheering

Cork Celtic 1969 Cup Final
COURTESY EXAMINER

19

for? Did I miss something?" "You did," was the reply. "You missed three goals. We're winning 4-3." Celtic eventually won 7-3. Donal got four and Frankie McCarthy got three. It was the costliest penny that centre-half ever spent.

Donal Leahy went on to work as assistant manager to both Paul O'Donovan with Cork Celtic and Tony Allen with Cork City but he admits that one of happiest periods in his career was when he was manager of Rockmount. Married with five daughters he has a quiet pride in the fact that two of them represented their country in athletics. Although he played all his life with Cork Celtic in Turner's Cross he points out that he started his career with a northside team, Dunbar Celtic, and ended it with a northside team, Rockmount. Once, when he was playing particularly well, he was told that if he agreed to sign for a certain Dublin club he would be immediately capped for Ireland, but he refused. I asked him if he had any regrets and he shook his head. "I had a long and happy innings," he smiled. "What more could any man want?"

Tomás MacCurtain

In the early 1920's Cork, the rebel county, a garrison town, was a cauldron of political passion. Most young men joined the Irish Volunteers and were constantly involved in minor skirmishes with the RIC. Secretly, they drilled out in the fields on the outskirts of the city, chopped down trees and blocked roads, dug trenches, delivered dispatches, quietly observed the enemy and generally played at being soldiers anxiously waiting for a war.

With each confrontation with the British Army, tension grew in every town in Ireland. People had grown tired of turning the other cheek. The next two years were to be the most traumatic in Irish history. It all reached boiling point in Cork during the spring of 1920. On 30th January, after a dramatic council meeting, Tomás MacCurtain was elected Cork's first Republican lord mayor but, sadly, his term of office was to last only seven weeks. At 1.15am on Saturday, 20th March, his thirty-sixth birthday, he was murdered in his home by Crown Forces. Members of the RIC, with blackened faces and socks pulled over their boots to muffle the sound, hammered on his front door and got his wife, Lizzie, out of bed. While two held her, their combrades ran up the stairs and shot MacCurtain in front of his young children. His assassins ran quickly off into the night and left him mortally wounded on the bedroom floor. His last words, in the arms of local priest, Fr Burts, were "Into thy hands, oh Lord, I commend my spirit." Word of the murder spread like wildfire. Rumour followed counter-rumour. People were frightened, confused and shocked.

That weekend Cork was a city of mourning. It was revealed that two days before his death the late Lord Mayor had received a threatening letter saying, "Prepare for death. You are doomed." It is interesting to note that the message was written on official Dáil Eireann notepaper, which suggests that British military intelligence had found ways and means of acquiring nationalist stationery. Typically, MacCurtain only laughed at this threat.

On the following Monday, Cork came to a standstill during the funeral: the docks were shut, factories and shops were closed and there were no trams or newspapers. The burial was at St Finbarr's Cemetery. There was a mounting anger in the city. MacCurtain's killers were instantly identified by local volunteers. They demanded revenge but the perpetrators had fled to different parts of the country. Divisional Inspector Swanzy of the RIC, who was allegedly one of the murderers, was transferred up north. He was tracked down to an RIC barracks in Lisburn. A First Cork Brigade man was given the job and, on 22nd August, as Swanzy left church, he died in a hail of bullets from MacCurtain's own personal revolver.

Tomás MacCurtain lying in state 1920.
COURTESY EXAMINER

Terence MacSwiney

The Black and Tans arrived in Ireland on 25th March 1920. At noon on the following Tuesday Terence MacSwiney was unamimously elected Lord Mayor of Cork. He was seconded by the famous volunteer Tom Barry. His first act in office was to give £250 of his £500 salary to a memorial fund for MacCurtain's widow.

The City Hall was packed on that Tuesday when he stood up before a hushed and expectant audience. They weren't disappointed. He began a long, emotional speech by eloquently stating: "I come hear more as a soldier stepping into the breach than an admisistrator," and he made the point that MacCurtain's murder was an attempt to terrify the country, and stressed that Irish people should show themselves completely and utterly unterrified. He finished with the immortal and often misused quotation: "It is not they who can inflict the most but they who can suffer the most will conquer." The tense gallery erupted in thunderous applause.

Terence MacSwiney realised only too well that his life was in danger. His friends wanted an armed guard with him day and night but he wouldn't hear of it. He felt he wouldn't be able to get his work done. Still, he hardly ever stayed in his own home. He and his friends came to an arrangement that he slept in a different house every night.

On the night of Thursday, 12th August 1920, the City Hall was surrounded and Terence MacSwiney, who often worked late in his office, was arrested. It was Daniel Corkery who broke the news to Muriel MacSwiney of her husband's arrest. The mayor was taken to Victoria Barracks in Dillon's Cross where he was court-martialled and found guilty of trumped-up charges and given two years in Brixton Prison. In protest, he immediately went on hunger-strike. For the next ten weeks the world watched while MacSwiney stubbornly refused to eat and, despite pleas from all sections of the community, he suffered a slow, painful death. The situation turned out to be a huge propaganda victory for the Republicans. On one day alone, forty thousand people in Cork said the Rosary by the National Monument and, on another day, thirty thousand English workers demanded his release. Sadly, it was not to be. On Monday, 25th October, after 74 days' fasting, he passed away.

When MacSwiney's body was eventually returned to Ireland from Brixton it was laid out in Cork's City Hall. Thousands filed by. They were shocked by the gaunt, hollow-cheeked features of the late Lord Mayor. His death had a huge effect on the city.

The removal of Terence MacSwiney from City Hall Cork.
COURTESY EXAMINER

The Burning of Cork

Surely 1920 was the most eventful year in the history of Cork City: the murder of Lord Mayor, Tomás MacCurtain, and the arrest, hunger-strike and death of his successor, Terence MacSwiney, brought a dramatic escalation of the tit-for-tat violence. The Black and Tans went berserk. In one week 24 towns were badly damaged, looted and burned, including Trim, Balbrigan, Fermoy, Ennistymon, Lahinch, Milltown Malbay and Mallow. On 21th November they fired recklessly into the crowd at a football match in Croke Park, killing twelve people including one player. A few days later, the First Cork Brigade, led by Tom Barry, ambushed a convoy at Kilmichael and killed 16 members of the British Army. But every time the Black and Tans were hit, they retaliated with a vengeance.

Then on Saturday night, 10th December, six volunteers attacked a lorry-load of Auxiliaries near Dillon's Cross, killing one before making their escape. The reaction by the Black and Tans was instant and savage. They swept into the city centre and, with drums of petrol, systematically

Cork the day after the burning.
COURTESY EXAMINER

25

burned building after building. Catholic shops took priority and the way certain premises were picked out and destroyed by different groups strongly suggests the attack was organised and prearranged. A tram was set on fire near Patrick's Bridge and the looting went on all through the night. The fire brigade were called but were fired on, and an ambulance carrying an injured fireman was spattered with bullets. The stench of smoke was everywhere. All through the night the Black and Tans continued to smash and loot pubs and shops as they made their way to the City Hall, the symbol of Republicanism. With the aid of sledgehammers they quickly broke down the doors. Tins of petrol, bombs and incendiary devices were swiftly ferried from the nearby Union Quay Barracks by their combrades. The bombs were strategically placed all over the building and soaked with petrol. The raiders ran to safety and, within minutes, the whole place was a blazing inferno. Symbolically, as the clock high up in the City Hall struck 6am, the entire dome gave way and crashed down, sending a spray of sparks into the dark night.

At first, the British blamed the IRA. Then they accused the people of burning their own city. The media stated that the City Hall caught fire and flames from this accidently set Patrick St ablaze. To back up this theory, an English newspaper printed a diagram of Cork with the City Hall conveniently relocated in Patrick St.

The next morning people flocked in from near and far to see the still-smouldering rubble. The effect was traumatic. They just stood and looked on in silent disbelief.

Cork the day after the burning.
COURTESY EXAMINER

Christy Ring
The first superstar

In modern times it is sad to see that money seems to have completely taken over in sport. Some golfers now demand appearance money even before they condescend to strike a ball, tennis players get huge sums of money for winning second-rate tournaments, and quite ordinary and robotic footballers are tranferred for millions of pounds. Money moguls pull the strings, commercialism reigns supreme and many big clubs are more like supermarkets. Words like superlative, megastar and awe-inspiring are commonly used to describe these "great" players.

Sometimes, in a reflective mood after an acute attack of nostalgia, I think back on players who unfortunately missed the sporting boat. One man especially, born before his time and surely the original superstar, is Cork hurler Christy Ring. Imagine if he was twenty-five years old and playing at the present time. The thought is mind-boggling. Not alone was he the most charismatic player of all time at his chosen sport but for a quarter of a century he was outstanding when the standard was at an extraordinary high level. To him it wasn't just a game. It was life itself. Without question, the period between 1949 and 1954 was the golden age of hurling. During these six years Cork and Tipperary clashed in the Munster championship. They were six titanic struggles fought out with an intense fervour, and the victors went on to win the all-Ireland title each time. Money was never an issue.

Memories flood back of our packed front room, wireless blazing forth, our collective hearts in our collective mouths, silently praying for a Cork victory as Michael O'Hehir, with his "sliothar dropping on the fourteen-yard line" and his "shemozzles in the goalmouth", held us in the palm of his hand. When television came it was a poor substitute. All the mystery disappeared.

In the fifties, it seemed to be an annual pilgrimage to Limerick to do battle with that great premier county team. Their full-back line - Byrne, Maher and Carey - had an awesome reputation. With the mercurial Tony Reddan behind them in goal they were like the Rock of Cashel. Nothing passed. Looking back subjectively, when Cork did score, I can still see the sliothar sailing over the bar while the Tip defenders wrapped their hurleys around their unfortunate opponents' necks and gently strangled them. And they seemed to enjoy it. It was blood and thunder stuff and not for the faint-hearted. They certainly raised them tough in Tipperary, and they could hurl, too. Then there was that colossus, John Doyle. It must have been like going through the Berlin Wall to find yourself being flattened by a Russian tank. Even Roy of the Rovers would have had his hands full, yet "Ringy" got many great goals in those games.

The return journey from Limerick was always special. Songs were sung, drink was drank and crubeens were unceremoniously demolished as we arrived home tired, hoarse and happy. Those magical of days of simple innocence are long gone.

I first met Christy Ring when I was eleven. We had won an under-twelve street league final and we were to go along to the Glen Hall to receive our trophies. It shows how poor a hurler I was by the fact that I was placed nineteenth in the waiting queue. One by one my team-mates went up. At last my turn came and, with legs like jelly, I nervously walked up the aisle, head down, hair over my face; I had hair then. As the great man shook my little hand two things stood out: one was his massive wrists and, secondly, he had the most unusual steel blue eyes which seemed to have a built-in twinkle. I'll never forget what he said to me: "Keep your eye on the ball even when it's in the referee's pocket". That night I floated home.

Will there ever be a more dramatic Munster final than that of 1956? I was a lonely, sensitive garsún listening to that match in my aunt's kitchen in Dublin. With ten minutes remaining Cork were being trashed by Limerick, and that fine hurler, Donal Broderick, was playing a blinder on Ring. Radio Eireann decided to switch over to the Ulster football decider. What a mistake. With despair in my heart and tears in my eyes I sat down and waited for the result: Limerick 3-5, Cork 5-5. I jumped up and, in my excitement, knocked cups and saucers all over the place. My aunt picked up a frying pan and gave me a bothering box across the back, but in my euphoria I didn't feel a thing.

"Ringy" had the actor's instinct for dramatic timing and his three goals in five minutes in that eventful game were pure genius. In hindsight Limerick hadn't a chance. Bishop Con Lucey threw in the ball and God was playing for Cork. Even today, the two most famous Limerick hurlers are Broderick and Mackey, but for contrasting reasons.

Come September and those giants from Wexford stood between Ring and his ninth all-Ireland medal. Memories from that thrilling game are sketchy: Ring's great tussle with Willie Rackard, his solo run and point followed by a goal which electrified the 83,000 crowd, Art Foley's late important save which got better and better as the years rolled by. I was quite near it and, on the day, I thought it was a very ordinary save but, admittedly, my objectivity was shrouded by rose-coloured glasses. I can still see "Ringy" charging in on the goalkeeper and the apprehensive Art Foley understandably hopping up and down on his goal line. But the great man just shook his hand and when the final whistle blew, in a lovely gesture of sporting reciprocation, the Wexford backs shouldered him like a king from Croke Park. Sadly, as Cork was to go through a barren ten-year patch, it was his last all-Ireland.

It is difficult to sum up all his hurling abilities. Once, when he was in his forties, he scored 6-4 in a game against Wexford. If you take Pele, Carl Lewis, Babe Ruth, Lester Piggot, throw in Arkle, add the strength of an ox and the cunning of a fox, then you have Christy Ring. He played with fire in his veins and a pride and passion in his performance. He was the only player in the world I would pay to see training. He tried the impossible. What other player would practice cutting the ball over the bar from behind the corner flag?

Ring going for his ninth medal against Wexford 1956.
COURTESY EXAMINER

29

At the age of sixteen, I cycled up to Limerick just to see him play. Ironically, he spoiled the game because I was watching only one player, and when he changed at the interval so did half the crowd. Wherever he appeared he doubled the attendances and when he stopped playing for Munster interest in the Railway Cup faded.

In Ring's era men were men and hard knocks were given, taken and forgotten. His likes will never be seen again and Cork is still craving for a hurling hero.

My irreverent children mock me when I polish my little silver "egg cup" which I received all those years ago in the Glen Hall. I ignore them because that night I met my God.

A friendly chat between Ring and Mackey 1957.
COURTESY JUSTIN NELSON, CLONMEL NATIONALIST

The Magical Movies

I will never forget my first visit to the magical world of the cinema. I was a tiny three year old, and I was sneaked in to St Mary's Hall under the shawl of a friendly neighbour. It shows the effect it had on me when I can still remember the film - The Fighting Sullivans. It was to be the beginning of a love affair with the cinema.

It is all so different now: Sky Movies, a variety of films screened practically 24 hours a day, the advent of the cineplex and video shops on every corner. Not so long ago Cork had a wide range of cinemas each with its own personality: the Savoy, Capitol, Pavillion, Ritz, Palace, Coliseum, Belle Vue, Lido, Assembley Rooms and Imperial (Miah's). For generations of Corkonians the Assems in the South Mall and Miah's in Oliver Plunket St had a colour and character all of their own. On one of my first visits to Miah's, downstairs was full. This wasn't surprising as it was like a big shoe box and it wouldn't take much to fill it. My older and more affluent brother brought me upstairs to the gallery. I couldn't get over my disappointment in finding it was the same screen as downstairs. I thought it would be much bigger and better for the extra three pence.

Miah's Cinema, Oliver Plunket Street.
COURTESY EXAMINER

Also, the projector on the back wall was very low and, every night, smart-Alecs kept putting their hands up to block the film at a crucial point.

Surely the Assems was the most popular venue for generations of filmgoers. If you survived the unmerciful crush to get in you'd get over anything. In many ways, the serials were the forerunner of the present day soaps. Each night, it ended with a dramatic cliff-hanger where the helpless heroine was in deadly danger. But, in the following episode, she was always saved by the handsome hero. Tarzan, Batman, Captain Marvel and Flash Gordon spring to mind.

St. Marys Hall Cinema on right facing North Cathedral.
Note extra houses on Shandon Street. These houses were demolished to make for Cathedral Road.

The slapstick comedy was also enjoyed with an animated relish: Bud Abbot and Lou Costello; Laurel and Hardy; the Marx Brothers and the Three Stooges.

But the most popular films by a mile were the westerns. You could safely say that every western was guaranteed audience participation. It was like an adult panto as the villian was booed and the hero was cheered to the rafters. If Johnny MacBrown was in danger he was saved by the anguished patrons: "Watch your back, Johnny." It worked every time. After all, he had to stay healthy so that, at the end, he could ride off into the sunset.

Georgie was one of the great characters of the Assems. He was the usher and was armed with a long, silver torch. When someone was shot in a film the deafening cry was: "Georgie, remove the body."

The star cowboys were: Lash Larue, Buck Jones, Tom Mix, Randolf Scott, Bill Boyd as Hopalong Cassidy, and Charles Starret as the Durango Kid. Charles Starret was my own favourite. I even wrote to him, but he never replied; another huge disappointment in my life. I once saw Bill Boyd throw in the ball to start a hurling match in Croke Park. I called out to him but he, too, never replied. Oh, the pain of youthful rejection. He was a frail, white-haired man. It was nearly half-time by the time he got to the sideline.

Without doubt, the westerns were the peoples' favourites. Many Corkonians fondly remember the simple innocence of those halcyon days. Sadly, it is an era which is long gone. Hopefully, it will never be forgotten.

Nancy McCarthy

Nancy McCarthy was a fascinating woman. The first time we met, many years ago, she was in a heated discussion with a priest over some religious disagreement. For an hour the argument waged to and fro until, eventually, the unfortunate priest threw his hands in the air in a gesture of defeat. "All right. All right, Nancy. I give up. You're right," he said in despair.

"I know I'm right, Father. I've been trying to tell you that for the last hour but you wouldn't listen," she answered in triumph.

Another day, I spotted her walking her beloved poodles near her home; at the time she was in her eighties. I crossed the Douglas Rd and hurried after her. It was a cold winter day and she was well muffled up against the wind.

"How are you, Nancy? You're looking great," I said.

She looked me up and down with a twinkle in her eye.

"I'm not looking great and well you know it," she said and strutted off like Helen of Troy and left me standing there in her wake. That was Nance.

Nancy McCarthy was once engaged to Cork writer, Frank O'Connor. After two years she decided to break it off. He got a nervous breakdown.

She first met him when she went along to audition for a play being staged by the Cork Drama League. Although she had a noticeable stammer she was both a fine singer and actress. She got the part. That night O'Connor walked her home. From then on she was his leading lady and she was to flit in and out of his life until the day he died.

That summer they went off to Donegal on a three-week holiday. She told her father that she was going with a friend without saying who the friend was. The poor man had ten children, and had enough on his mind, so the youngsters went away all alone. The holiday was a disaster. They stayed in houses three miles apart, it never stopped raining, and they were continuously drenched.

After a month she was brought up to the Barrack Stream to be shown off to his mother. Minnie was very wary of this new girl in her son's life. She made cocoa and biscuits for them and discreetly disappeared.

Nancy was a daily communicant. For 18 months she met O'Connor every day outside St Peter and Paul's church after mass. He proposed to her over a hundred times, but although she loved him, she just would not marry him.

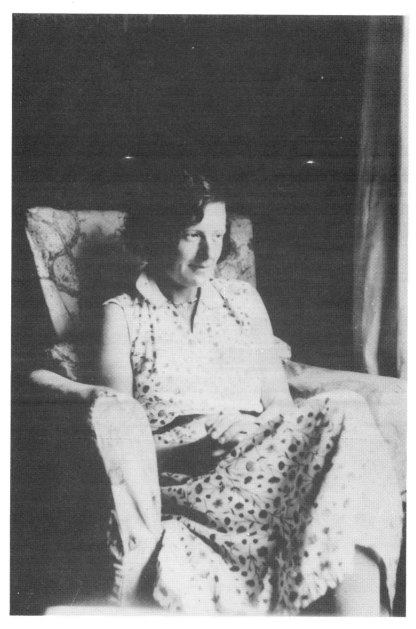

Nancy McCarthy
COURTESY HARRIET SHEEHY

She had a razor-sharp intelligence and was incredibly active. She ran a busy chemist shop and was involved in theatre, music, the Cork International Film Festival and the Cork Ballet Company all her life. Although she took up mountaineering very late in life, she became a more than capable climber. Once, she came across a man halfway up a steep mountain. Undaunted, she climbed over him and carried on regardless. Typically, the night before she died she visited an art gallery.

In October 1988 I called at her bungalow to see her. We had a cup of tea, a slice of brown bread and a long cosy chat. Her front room was like a shrine to O'Connor. As we talked about him for hours, her face glowed with affection and she kindly showed me dozens of old poems and love letters he had written to her and she played tapes and records of his voice. She was clearly in love with him all her life and before I left I got up the courage to ask her one last question.

"Nancy, why didn't you marry him?"

She was quiet for a moment.

"There was sickness in the family at the time."

She was looking out the window as she spoke almost to herself. What she said was quite true. Her mother had been very ill for long periods and Nancy had a genuine fear that there might be a touch of insanity in the family. O'Connor, who was aware of this, cheered her up one day when he put his arm around her and said, "You know, Mac, you were always afraid of insanity but, by God, you're the sanest damn person I know."

Their personalities were similar in many ways: both were singleminded and stubborn and, although she loved him dearly, she may have been wise enough to realise that their marriage may not have survived on a long-term basis.

That night was my last time seeing this lovely lady. She died the following week and surprised everyone by having her remains cremated. She told a friend, "I don't want the pigeons to be talking about me." She had arranged to have her ashes scattered in her beloved Dunquin on the rugged County Kerry coast. Friends turned up from all over the world to pray and watch as her ashes dissolved in the wild Atlantic Ocean in a simple but moving ceremony. It was typical of her that she left strict instructions that the 'scatterin' was to take place only when the wind was blowing out to sea. She didn't want the ashes to blow into the faces of anyone in Cork.

Afterwards, everyone retired to Kruger's hostelry in Dunquin where, naturally, the conversation turned to Nancy. Each story was followed by another. One friend recalled the day Nancy was caught in a hail of bullets during the Civil War and dived for cover behind a wall. When a Free Stater asked her if she was afraid of being shot, she said indignantly, "No, 'tis playing marbles I was." It was common knowledge that she got great pleasure from the fact that the Civil War was put on hold for ten minutes every morning while the milkman delivered milk to her house near Monkstown. The evening ended with one final toast to "Herself." It was only right that Nancy McCarthy had become part of the elements, as befitting such a free spirit.

She is in heaven now scattering sunshine and dancing with the angels.

An older Nancy McCarthy with her beloved poodles.
COURTESY EXAMINER

John Delea

John Delea is with Rockmount Football Club almost forty years. He made his debut with the under 12 team in 1960 and so began a life-long love affair with the club. Affectionately known as 'Billy Bremner' because of his likeness to the late, great Leeds' player. "I was a fiery midfielder with a mop of curls then," he recalls. Eventually, he made it on to the junior team but a broken leg interrupted his progress. Then a serious eye injury finished his career and he became a member of the committee at the very young age of 21. He was now managing the under 16 team and, in 1972, they won their first schoolboy trophy - the under 16 league. The floodgates were well and truly opened. John moved on to managing the minor team and 1975 was an eventful year in more ways than one. "We had a fine minor team and we won the shield, league and Murphy Cup,

Tom O'Callaghan and John proudly hold the Intermediate Cup.

but we were playing a lot of evening matches and I was having a problem getting off work. At the time I had a great job in Dunlops but every second week I was on four to midnight. There was only one thing I could do. I left the job. When I went home and told my father he wouldn't believe me. 'You gave up the best job in Cork for football,' he said. The poor man nearly collapsed with the shock."

John was also selector of the Cork AUL minors and they won the cup three years in a row - 1973/74/75. He remembers some of the lighter moments: Rockmount were being beaten 5-1 by Temple up in Knocknaheeny. Castleview and Central were also playing. A heavy fog came down and the referee abandoned the match late on in the game. At the AUL meeting on the following Wednesday night the abandoned game was being discussed. The Castleview delegate stood up and said that he couldn't see the goalposts with the fog. The Central man said that he couldn't see the corner flag. Not to be outdone, the Rockmount delegate jumped up and said, "With a quarter of an hour to go I put on the twelth man and I didn't see him since." Another time there was an important meeting called to discuss ways and means of fundraising.

John with Brian Robson.

Over thirty players and committee attended and everyone gave their opinion how money could be raised. Some were in favour of a big raffle. Others suggested a weekly draw and someone else wanted a sponsored walk. One frustrated young lad who was centre-forward on the youths team made his contribution. "Mr Chairman, there's no balls coming in from the wing."

By now Rockmount had the best youth players in the country and a certain young Roy Keane appeared on the scene. When he was nine he was voted under 11 player of the year, and that team was unbeaten in Munster for the next six years. In 1988, when John was assistant manager, the 17 year-old Roy came under his wing. He played eight senior games with Rockmount before moving on to Cobh Ramblers and the rest is history. I knew I was putting John on the spot when I asked him to name his best eleven Rockmount players. "It's impossible," he said. "I could name a hundred. In fact, one or were equally good prospects as Roy. Paul

Two Fiery Midfielders – John and Pat Crerand.

40

McCarthy captained the Irish under 21 team and went to Brighton. We had dozens of players who were capped. There was Len Downy, Alan O'Sullivan, Jimmy Nodwell, Ritchie Noonan, Aidan O'Mahony, Jason Lynch. I could go on all night." But you could tell that Roy was special. "When he went to Forest I used to go over to a lot of games. He usually met me at the airport and I stayed in his house. Since he signed for United I travel over regularly. He always picks me up at the airport and I have my own special room in his house. He even gave me my own key and nobody bothers me. Yes, Roy is very special."

John Delea is proud that he is chairman of Rockmount this year - their 75th anniversary - and what a way to celebrate the event. "Winning the Intermediate Cup and Munster Senior League is the club's greatest acchievement and we have a fine young team which will only improve. Some mornings I wake up and I still can't believe we are the Intermediate Cup holders."

In the semi-final, in Cork, against Swilly Rovers it was a draw with time almost up. John, who was about to have a serious operation, was dreading the expense of a replay in Donegal. He turned away, looked to the heavens, and prayed quietly to himself. "I don't care about the operation but God, please God, give us a goal." He must have had a good

John with Ryan Giggs, The Welsh Wizard.

41

line to the Almighty. Within seconds Kieran O'Shea got the ball and crashed it into the net. The full-time whistle went, and Rockmount went on to beat Gárda in the final.

And all this by a club which started from humble beginnings in 1924. They were named after Rockmount House - a house in the Commons Rd. Their pitch and facilities in Whitechurch are now second to none. But all this didn't happen overnight. Down through the years the likes of Tom O'Callaghan, Harry Pegler, John Twomey, John and Vincie Cummins, Denis O'Donovan, Jimmy Deasy, Teddy and Tony Barry, Tommy Hosford, John O'Shea and the late Neilus Joyce worked tirelessly and unselfishly for the club. I asked John what the future held for him; would he retire? He laughed at the suggestion. "Even my dog is called Rocky after the club. I'll stay with them till I die," he said. "Sure Rockmount are my life."

Three Stout Corkmen

Pawnshops

In the early fifties there were 18 pawnbrokers in Cork City - four in Shandon St alone. These shops were easily identified by the three golden balls hanging high above the entrances. One Cork wag said, "Two to one you won't get your own back."

It is doubtful if anyone under the age of thirty would be familiar with the function of the pawnbroker. Yet, in the middle of this century, they were an integral part of working-class Cork. There were three even situated in what could be called the inner city: two on Lavitt's Quay near the Opera House; another at the bottom of Patrick's Hill.

In many ways they were the poor mans' bank. It was unheard of then for someone in need to go to a bank. The alterative was a moneylender or a pawn. The latter was by far the lesser of two evils. To some families, living on the breadline, they were a godsend - the only way to survive. It was a weekly ritual. First thing on Monday morning some item, from a mundane piece of jewelry to an article of clothing, was pawned (put in hock). The most popular items were: men's suits, shoes, blankets, furniture, tradesmen's tools, watches, wedding rings and clocks. After much haggling, the money received for these had to cover the family needs for the week. Come Saturday - the pawn opened late on Saturday - if the wife was lucky enough to get a wage, she paid the fee plus the interest, and redeemed the item. It was often her husband's suit to enable him to go to mass on Sunday. Then, on Monday morning, the whole process began again.

Jones' Pawnshop, Shandon Street –
Corks last pawn.
COURTESY EXAMINER

43

The pawnbroker was a much maligned and often unfairly criticised man. Although he knew that he always had to get his money - he sold the goods if he didn't - he had to be a businessman to survive. Yet, at times, he also had to be a psycologist and a good judge of character. When some regular clients had gained his confidence, after numerous transactions, they sometimes used underhand methods to obtain their porter money. One such character often pawned his box of tools. This caused another problem. With no tools, he couldn't go to work. But neccessity is the mother of invention. He continued to pawn his tool-box but the tools were removed and replaced by two bricks. The unfortunate pawnbroker never suspected. Another man regularly pawned his suit. It was well wrapped in brown paper and his young son religiously handed the parcel over the counter with the instructions: "The usual, sir." This meant £2. This practice went on for years until one day, when the family were leaving the area, the boy was sent on his usual errand. He handed over the parcel and duly received the £2. When the pawnbroker checked the contents, after a year, he discovered a mouldy old blanket. These two hardy souls were drinking in a pub one day when they ran out of money. One of them noticed a beautiful overcoat, belonging to the proprietor, hanging up in the corner. While he acted as a decoy his friend paid a flying visit to the nearby pawn, got a fine sum for the coat, and the thirsty twosome drank away to their hearts' content. Hours later they handed the pawn docket to the puzzled bar owner, staggered out the door and were never seen again.

It is now 25 years since the last pawn closed down for good - Jones' shop at the bottom of Shandon St. It was the end of an era. The writing was on the wall with the introduction of hire purchase. The arrival of the credit union in the late fifties combined with the exodus of families to the sprawling housing estates on the outskirts of the city finally put an end to the pawnbroker. They were of another time and a grim reminder of the poverty of the forties and fifties.

Nowadays the Celtic Tiger is roaring and it's a common sight to see a queue of teenagers outside a bank with a plastic card in one hand and a mobile phone in the other.

The Buttera

Two of the oldest and most famous bands in the country were founded on opposite sides of the River Lee - the Barrack St and Butter Exchange Bands. They are intrinsically linked with Cork and, for over a century, there has been a friendly rivalry and a mutual respect for each other.

The Butter Exchange Band (the Buttera) was established in 1878 in one of the most historic parts of the city. Down through the years their standard was considered to be so high that the band has been a constant nursery for the army school of music. They have been hugely successful in brass band competitions and have a string of awards to their name. For decades they have been renowned for their generosity and they regularly give their services at charity functions.

In their long history there were many well-known conductors. Jack Marshall was the most famous. The present conductor is Herbie Hendrick who has been with the band for almost fifty years. The Buttera has added colour and excitement to many important events and has provided the entertainment before countless sporting occasions. They played outside the City Hall for the visit of President Kennedy in 1963, and the band was mentioned by Bloom in James Joyce's famous book, Ulysses. I remember them playing a blinder at the opening of Páirc U° Chaomh, and for years they gave a two-hour recital on Sunday afternoons at the bandstands on the Marina and the Mardyke.

Although bands take their music very seriously, down through the years there has been the odd mishap. The trombone section, because of the nature of the instrument, usually lead the band while marching. During one parade in a town in West Cork, a trombone player lost control of his slide. It flew past the surprised conductor. The musician bent down to pick up his slide and the band continued to march over their unfortunate colleague. Under the stage of the old Opera House there was an earthen floor. To avoid boredom and help pass the time some bandsmen often brought along their golf clubs and practiced their putting. It is a well-known fact that musicians have been known to have a fondness for alcohol. It was a common sight in the old Opera House to witness some band members dash out the stage door, into the nearby pub, down a quick drink and, with perfect timing, flash back right on cue with seconds to spare. They were expert at counting the bars of music. They took it in turns to count the bars which worked every time in rehearsals, but on the opening night the musician whose turn it was to

46

count was distracted by an old drinking combrade and lost the count. Back in the pit when the conductor put his baton up for a blazing fanfare he was met by an embarrassing silence. It is said that the modern day musician now uses a mobile phone.

It is interesting to note that several showband stars learned their trade with the Butter Exchange Band: Barry and Herbie Hendrick, Seán Lucey, Theo Cahill and Joe McCarthy. With the surge of young female membership in recent years there is a bright future ahead.

The Buttera has every reason to blow its own trumpet. They aim to continue to be the musical heartbeat of the Northside for many years to come.

The Barracka

The Barrack St Band (Barracka) was founded by Fr Mathew in 1837. It is the oldest band in Ireland. Cork at that time was a thriving city of over 80,000 people.

In 1842 the band had an early claim to fame when it played to a thronged city centre audience as Daniel O'Connell and Fr Mathew strolled side by side down the South Mall. Several band members were supporters of Daniel O'Connell and often joined him when he spoke at demonstrations. There was a massive crowd of 500,000 people at one such gathering. Later, these passionate political get-to-gethers got a bit heated and sometimes ended up in disarray.

In the course of the following century, the Barrack St Band has held a unique place in Cork's musical history. The legendary Bobby Lambe was first put through his paces in that famous bandroom. Down the years, they have graced many sporting venues: Munster Finals, the FAI Cup Final and Ireland v Liverpool at Flower Lodge, and they led the parade when Cork won the All-Ireland senior double in 1990.

Paddy O'Callaghan, one of the best men at the helm, has stood down and handed over the reins to the present conductor, Keven Meldrum. Typically, Kevin has come right up through the ranks and with his guidance they are All-Ireland Champions for the last two years. In 1992 a highly successful youth and education policy was introduced. Now there are as many as 40 youngsters studying and many go on to join the prestigious Irish Brass Band. Like their Northside counterparts, the Barracka can face the future with great confidence.

49

John O'Driscoll
The Man with the Magic Hands

" We were destroying Blackrock 3-0 in Church Rd one Sunday. It was only at half-time when Christy McGrath was giving out the oranges that we discovered 12 players had played for us in the first half. One player was sneaked off, and nothing was said. Imagine that happening today."

It's hard to believe that Johnny O'Driscoll is nearly 90. One hour in his company is like a 75 year stroll down Cork's sporting history. He paints a kaleidoscope of anecdotes.

Wembley soccer club and Sunnyside boxing club have been the two loves of his life. Coincidently, both clubs were named after pubs; the Wembley Bar in McCurtain St and the Sunnyside off Blarney St.

"Church Road was the Mecca of football in Cork for decades and, one way or another, you always got great entertainment. Not everyone could afford boots. The pitch was in a terrible condition during this particular game. These two team-mates could never agree. 'You're a handy player,' shouted one, 'wearing your good shoes on a day like this.' His pal shouted back, 'They're not mine. They're yours'. At another game time was almost up when the ball went out of play. This well-known player, with particularly poor eyesight, ran after it, picked up a crash helmet by mistake, threw it to a team-mate and knocked him out cold. Footballs weren't as plentiful then as they are now. Sometimes there might be only one ball at a game, and this could cause problems. One man, whose team were losing, picked up his ball and went home. The other team were still awarded the match. In a similar situation, during another game, an attempt was made to puncture the ball with a scissors when it went wide. Instead, the goalkeeper was stabbed in the leg and had to go to hospital. They were up to all kinds of tricks. There weren't many teams around then but the standard was extremely high. Not alone did every team have several fine players but they also had great characters. And the referees were often even more colourful - Nedser Cotter comes to mind. In Church Rd, again, he was getting a bad time from this supporter who was wearing a then trendy Robin Hood hat. Nedser eventually blew his whistle and confronted the man. 'Hey, Robin, you and your merry men better get out of here quick or I'll abandon the game'. Another well-known referee had taken enough backchat from a player. He produced his notebook. 'Name, please'? 'Roy Rogers', the player said. The referee

John O'Driscoll

51

didn't bat an eyelid as he wrote it down. 'Right, Roy. Get up on your horse and ride out of here. You're off'."

Johnny reminisced on how dramatically sport and life has changed in the last 20 years. He has to laugh when he sees players turning up for games now with several pairs of boots - each pair for different conditions. He remembers being involved in a tournament in the southside in the early thirties. There were two stones for the goals, four to mark the pitch, and the referee had to do everything: decide on corners, throw-ins and whether the ball was under or over the non-existent crossbar. Players had no boots and sometimes had to go to the pawnshop for a pair. They cost two shillings (10p), and you often got two odd boots. They were very well used by the time they were returned. Cardboard was stuffed down your stockings and used as shinguards. A ball for training was out of the question, but a pig's bladder was always available at the slaughterhouse. This did the trick.

I asked him what players sprang to mind in all his time with Wembley. I knew that it was an impossible question.

"It's very hard," he said. "There were so many. Billy Neville went to West Ham and played for Ireland. John Crowley had great skill and Nipper Murphy was a genius. He could make the ball talk. Later on there was Donie Connors, Patsy McCormack could have gone to Newcastle, Nelius Cronin went to West Brom, Gus Walsh played on the same Irish schoolboy team as Liam Brady, Paddy Short was outstanding and, of course, Tony Hennessy had everything. Arsenal wanted to sign Tony."

I had to laugh when he told me that the Gunners would have done anything to keep him. They even offered to give him a special large mirror so that he could comb his hair. At the time the Gunners had several English internationals on their books and Tony felt that he was as good as any of them. And I'm inclined to agree with him. Tony was a perfectionist. He used to climb over the railings of Fitzgerald Park at 7am every morning to train.

Johnny O'Driscoll recalls the good old days of boxing with equal affection. "There were some ferocious scraps in the Mechanics' Hall in the Marsh." he said. By all accounts, he was a mighty man to have in your corner. He trained future greats Séamus Cummins and Tommy Hyde when they were both six and a half stone, and he was in Sketchy Roche's corner for a professional bout against Mossie Condon. The rules stated that anyone in a pro's corner was automatically suspended for life but, in Johnny's case, the Munster Council turned a blind eye. He was too good to lose. More honours were to follow. London beckoned when he was specially invited to do Randy Turpin's corner. Turpin went on to beat Sugar Ray Robinson who is reckoned by many to be the greatest fighter who ever lived.

"Long ago the tournaments seemed to go on all night and they were full of passion and glamour. One night these two boxers were punching lumps out of each other. A ringside journalist was very worried. 'Someone will be killed,' he said. A spectator behind him, who had his codding cap on, whispered in his ear, 'They're fighting over the one woman and they're going to finish it in the ring.' The naive journalist was very impressed, and the morning headline said: TWO LOVERS FIGHT TO DEATH. There was no woman. The boxers weren't even jaggin'."

Johnny has a gifted pair of hands. He has been a masseur for 72 years. This incredibly generous man refuses no one - any person, any injury, any sport. Very often, after just one session, people have found miraculous relief even though doctors and hospitals had failed to help them. Down through the years he has been masseur to a wide range of teams: Munster youths in Germany which included Cork City's Dave Barry and Liam Murphy, and Liverpool's Jim Beglin; Irish junior team in Coventry; Cork youths in Bermingham; Blackrock hurling team; Mayfield hurling and football teams(they won everything that year); and the Ballyhea hurling team beaten by St Finbarr's in the county final. One official said that if they had won that game they would have built a statue to Johnny.

He is still an incredibly active man. A few years ago he made his stage debut when he took the part of a judge in a play, and for the following two years played the part of Herod in a Passion Play - Spencer Tracey eat your heart out. He goes dancing twice a week and recently, at a certain hotel, he was so impressive that he was asked up on stage, and proceeded to give a performance that Fred Astaire would have been proud of.

Johnny has the unique distinction of receiving the Cork Hall of Fame award for both boxing and soccer. It is richly deserved. Most of his life has been blessed with good health but, once, he had to attend the North Infirmary with arthritis in his knee. During the examination the doctor, a German, mentioned that his back was strapped up. Johnny said, "You fix my knee and I'll fix your back." A passing man asked the doctor if was treating Johnny. The doctor replied that he was. The man said, "Sure Johnny cured half of Cork." He wasn't far wrong.

Women's Jail

In 1810 it was decided that the prison near the North Gate Bridge was far too old and a new one was badly needed. A site was chosen high over the city in Convent Ave, Sundays Well, and work commenced in 1820 on what is now known as the Women's Jail. After two years a carpenters' strike stopped progress for several weeks. The building was eventually completed in 1824 and the first batch of prisoners arrived in June of that year. It cost 60,000 pounds - a huge amount of money for that time.

The majority of inmates were jailed for petty crimes: stealing bread, clothing, a pig or a sheep. The hungry and poor were shown no mercy. One nine year old boy got three weeks for stealing two plumbers' brass ball-cocks. He was whipped twice a week and then sent to a reformatory school for five years. Another young woman was sentenced to seven years for stealing cloth.

The first hanging was on Saturday 26th April, 1828. Owen Ryan was found guilty of assaulting a woman near the Lough and he was

Women's Jail
COURTESY RICHARD T. COOKE

sentenced to hang. The execution was right outside the front gate. A large crowd witnessed this but the hanging was botched and the unfortunate Mr Ryan took 20 minutes to choke to death.

In 1851 almost 3,500 inmates were incarcerated here. It became a jail solely for women in 1878. Male prisoners were marched over to the County Jail off the Western Rd which is now part of UCC.

Down through the years it has held many well-known political prisoners: Terence Bellew McManus, Isaac and Ralph Varian, James Mountaine, Denny Lane, John Sarsfield Casey, Brian Dillon, Frank O'Connor and Countess Markievicz.

During the Civil War in 1923 republican prisoners were interned here while awaiting sentence. Many were taken out and shot at the back of the prison. Conditions were dreadful: tiny cells, earthen floors, if it rained they got soaked, rats everywhere, and cold food. The main meal was 14oz of brown bread and two pints of milk. Solitary confinement was in a narrow, dark cell where prisoners were fed only bread and water. Some went insane in this two and a half foot hell. Others committed suicide by jumping from the high gallery. Nets had to be installed to prevent this practice. The only view the prisoners had was the unmarried mothers working in the fields below in the adjoining Good Shepherd Orphanage. The girls, in turn, used to wave up at the far-off faces barely visible behind bars.

In November 1923, forty-two prisoners dramatically escaped by tying bed clothes together and climbing over the high wall. Some were never seen again.

When the prison was first built there were mounds of leftover stones lying around for some months. The prison staff was mainly Protestant and, as their nearest place of worship was Shandon, it was decided to erect a church for them. But a Catholic priest, Fr McCarthy, stepped in and used the stones to build Strawberry Hill school - Cork's first national school. The school opened in 1835 and, ironically, it was Frank O'Connor's first school. He attended from September 1907 to June 1910.

In 1927 Cork Broadcasting Station (6CK) took over the building and, for the next 31 years, this station was a great source of entertainment for the people of Cork. It must be remembered that there was no recording then. Every programme went out live. The station closed down in 1958 when RTE opened its new headquarters in Union Quay.

The Dept of Posts and Telegraphs took over the prison mainly as a storage base and training centre, but during the next 30 years the building gradually fell into poor condition - the roof was now completely gone.

Then, in June 1993, mainly through the efforts of Diarmuid Kenneally, work began on replacing the roof and refurbishing the whole prison. Now, 175 years on, it is a beautiful new heritage centre sitting proudly over the city and tourists flock from the four corners of the world to visit and experience the colourful atmosphere of this historic building.

Honouring Brian Dillon who spent some time in the Women's Jail.
COURTESY EXAMINER

Connie Creedon

Connie Creedon, father of one of the most famous families in Cork, died on January 3rd 1999. He was 79 years old. For generations his shop, the Inchigeela Dairy, has been a well-known landmark in Cork City. Connie's father was also a shopkeeper. He collected the butter around the Inchageela/Ballingeary area many years ago and then delivered it to Cork via the butter road.

Connie's wife, Siobhán, died in 1986. The couple have twelve children - eight girls and four boys. Some are household names: John is presenter of RTE's Risin' Time; Conal is the writer of popular radio soap Under the Goldie Fish; Blake is an Examiner journalist; Geraldine is the creator of the memorial to Rory Gallagher in Paul's Square; and Nora was artistic director of the National Sculpture Factory and is now administrator of the Temple Bar Gallery. Connie was equally proud of all his children. An ex-pupil of the North Monastery, he was a charming yet extremely modest man. Although an avid sportsman all his life, he hadn't much spare time for matches as he worked hard to rear his family. He spent long hours on the road driving trucks and buses to every corner of Ireland.

Since moving to Bray to live with his daughter, Nora, he had become a huge fan of Cork City soccer team. Generally accompanied by his son, John, he rarely missed a match. The highlight was last years cup final win, and he even travelled to Switzerland to support them. The last three matches he attended must have given him immense pleasure - victories over Rovers, Waterford and Sligo. He was a great fan of goalkeeper, Noel Mooney, but Patsy Freyne was his particular favourite. Typically, after his last game, Patsy heard that Connie was in a certain bar so he made it his business to call there. On seeing his idol, Connie jumped up and hugged him like a schoolboy hugs his hero. Apathy was not a word in his vocabulary. He lived life to the full and had the unbridled enthusiasm of a child at Christmas.

Connie Creedon died as the train pulled in to Heuston Station. There is almost a sporting symbolism in his passing. He died "on the road" but more important, with three points in the bag for his beloved Cork City. His funeral was a happy event; there was no sadness. It was a celebration of a wonderful life. In a moving gesture the packed attendance gave him a standing ovation. He would have liked that.

In recent years he spent a lot of time with his son, John. "We had one thing in common," John said. "We were completely different. He was more like a younger brother than a father. One weekend we went off to a town in the West of Ireland and eventually ended up in a packed pub well after hours. There was no need to worry; the place was full of guards. In the early hours of the morning I felt tired and wanted to go to bed, but himself wanted to stay up and watch a big fight on the telly at five am. I warned him not to wake me. I like peace and quiet, curtains pulled and lights out. And I knew that he preferred bright lights, windows opened and radio blazing. Hours later I was awakened by someone at my feet moaning,'Whist, whist.' I put out my hand and felt Con's bald head. He thought he was at home and, in the darkness, tripped and banged his head on the telly. I picked him up like a big baby and put him in to bed." Connie had a grand turn of phrase. Once, they were in Bray on their way to a match in Waterford. John, who was driving, was worried about making the game on time. His father just smiled and said, "We'll be there in two skids and a jam on."

One busy Christmas, while serving in the shop, a man robbed half a dozen apples and ran off. Later, well after midnight, when Con was in bed, there was a knock on the front door. He opened up to discover the very man, the worse for wear, his pockets full of apples, looking for a bag for his ill-gotten fruit. He had gone off drinking for the night and didn't remember where he had stolen the apples. Connie was aware of this yet, typically, he gave him a bag, wished him a happy Christmas, and sent him on his merry way.

Connie Creedon was a lovely, gentle man and is sadly missed by his family and wide circle of friends. No doubt he is in heaven as personal chauffeur to the Almighty or happily dropping the apostles from cloud to cloud in his beloved bus.

Charlie McCarthy

Charlie McCarthy will go down as one of the greatest corner-forwards of all time. He would be on the short list for any hurling team from any era. Born in Tower St, he went to school in the South Convent before moving on to that renowned GAA nursery, Sullivan's Quay. Although his father, Jack, played with Redmond's and lined out with Cork, it was his mother who was the driving force behind him. She was an out and out GAA fanatic, and she strongly encouraged her son to play hurling.

"In reality Tyrone Place at the top of Tower St was only a small yard," Charlie remembers. "Yet it was our Croke Park. We played everything there - morning, noon and night."

As he got older he graduated to Hozzie's field off Friar's Walk where Deer Park is now situated. His first success came at eight, nine and ten in the Lough Parish League. Then, like his father, he joined Redmond's and, at eleven, he was playing with the under 15 team.

"Funnily enough," he recalls, "looking back at old photographs, I was the biggest player in the team then. I think I stopped growing when I was fifteen."

He first wore the Cork jersey for the under 15 team at 13 years of age. He now played with St Finbarr's and went on to represent Cork at minor hurling for three years in a row. Charlie was also an accomplished footballer and he nearly did the minor double in 1964: he won an All-Ireland hurling medal against Laois but Offaly got the better of Cork in the football decider. That Offaly team, which included the likes of Tony McTeague and Willie Bryan, was to dominate the senior football scene through the early seventies.

"I suppose 1966 was the most memorable year in my sporting career. First we had three titanic games against Wexford before we won the under 21 final in Croke Park. You must remember that the county hadn't won a senior All-Ireland for 12 years. That's an eternity for Cork. We had a very young team and were up against Kilkenny in the final. The experienced Noresiders were the favourites but, after a fiercely contested game, we were lucky enough to get there by a few points. Colm Sheehan from Éire Óg was the hero with three goals. Looking back at the video, recently, it was ferociously tough match."

There were strong rumours at the time that the Kilkenny team were allegedly given sleeping tablets to relax them on the night before the game and this affected their performance.

Charlie was a prolific marksman at every level. He scored a goal and nine points against Wexford in the 1970 final, and in the Munster minor semi-final in 1964 he scored 3-8 against Waterford. But one season his form suffered and it had nothing to do with hurling. The Irish Government brought out a huge anti-smoking television advertisement. Different sporting personalities like Steve Heighway, Mick O'Connell and Charlie were chosen to remind the nation about the danger of cigarettes. Charlie was once a light smoker but had seen the light and given them up. By now he was a household name, and a star of the small screen, and any time he played he was under even more pressure. When things weren't going his way in a game the crowd would shout, "Charlie, go back on the fags."

He played with and against some outstanding hurlers. He greatly admires Jimmy Doyle, Mick Roche and Eddie Keher, and John Gleeson

Charlie leading Jimmy Barry-Murphy and Cork
to victory in the 1978 All-Ireland Final.

60

and Jim Treacy were tremendous opponents. "Any time I played against Treacy I got a terrible slagging," he said. "Everyone kept telling me that I couldn't beat an old man. Jim had a head of grey hair but he was only about 23."

Charlie McCarthy has had a long and distinguished career. He won five All-Ireland medals and lost two to Kilkenny, five National Leagues, six hurling county medals and lost two football, one Railway Cup medal and three All-stars - 1972, '77 and '78 when he captained Cork to victory. Yet it was an achievement by his son which gave him most pleasure. Cathal plays senior hurling with St Finbarr's and has represented his county at under-age level. In 1998 he captained Cork to win the minor All-Ireland. Charlie was at the game. "It's a special feeling seeing your son being presented with the All-Ireland trophy," he said. "Yes, that was magic."

Charlie flanked by celebrities,
Roy Jenkins, President of the EEC and Mossie Keane

61

Séamus Cummins
Man of Steel

Down through the years Cork has had many sporting greats. Surely, Séamus Cummins was one of the most colourful. He boxed during and after the Second World War when the standard was at an all-time high. It was the time of the "hungry" fighter and a boxer had to be tough mentally and physically to survive. Yet, amazingly, Séamus never wore a gumshield.

"Well, I was hard to hit," he smiled.

The fact that he was never knocked out, and is still sharp and articulate, proves his point. In one fight, against Ron Pudney in London, one ringside

Séamus in his early 20s.

correspondent praised his "general ring craft and spectacular footwork."

Séamus Cummins was born in 1926 - the same year his father, James, a sergeant major in the Irish Army, played in goal for Kildare in the famous All-Ireland final against Kerry. Fifteen years later he reached the semi-final of the National Juvenile Championship. In 1942 he followed his father's footsteps and joined the army and, for the next two years, never lost a fight. Getting restless, he enlisted in the British Army and, over the next twelve months, again won every fight. During the army championships he fought six bouts in one day.

"I always kept myself fit," he said. "But I could punch, too. Most of my fights rarely went the distance. Funnily enough, although I trained very hard, the only time I saw the ring was when I fought."

He then transferred to the RAF where he remained unbeaten, overall, for four and a half years. In 1946, at just 20 years of age, he took the plunge and turned professional calling himself Tommy O'Connor. For the next two years he fought the best middleweights in Britain. It was exciting but the money wasn't great; you got £75 if you were top of the bill and won. This was very rare. Early on in his career a London

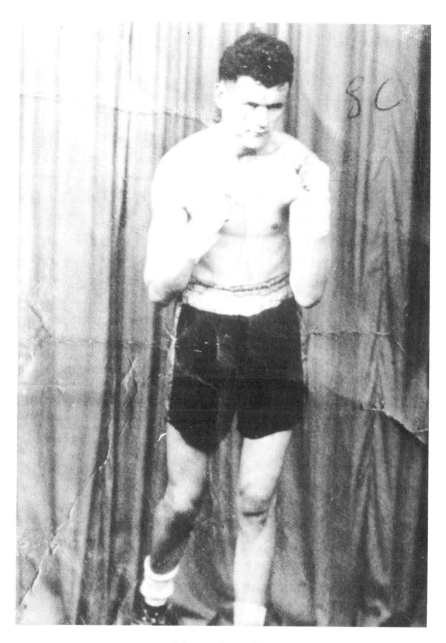

Séamus in action.

63

journalist forecast great things for him: "The undoubted power of the Irishman's right hand will bring him a long way."

His mother got a little October flower blessed by a priest and sent it on to her son. He used to stick it down his stocking as a lucky omen. It seemed to work; he won twelve in a row carrying the flower but then lost it for his thirteenth, and lost the fight.

"Bob Cleaver was very good but my hardest fights were against Ron Grogan. I beat him twice on points and the crowd were on their feet for the last three rounds shouting, 'Come on, Lovely Cottage'. That was a famous Irish horse at the time. I had one very unusual fight in Wembley; that night the film star, Stewart Grainger, was in my corner as a publicity stunt. It turned out to be a great scrap against Bernard Murphy, the Welsh champion.

Séamus' record speaks for itself: 25 fights in two years, losing only two on points, both very close decisions.

He returned home for good in 1948 and trained regularly with the likes of Sketchy Roche, Paddy Martin, Tommy Hyde, Peter Kenneally and Jimmy Hourigan. He always looked after himself and got great pleasure in the fact that, at the age of 58, he sparred a few rounds with the then Irish champion, Kieran Joyce.

"I'll tell you something. They didn't come any tougher than Jimmy Hourigan. We were supposed to be having a friendly spar one night but it got out of hand and became a bit heated. A shocked official kept shouting, 'Will ye stop, for God's sake. This is not a bullring'. Which reminds me how serious Jimmy took his training. He used to eat raw stake before walking out the countryside to wrestle with a bull. The bull lost every time."

Séamus received the boxing Hall of Fame Award in 1991 and he feels that people often forget about the importance of our administraters. He has fond memories of Charlie Atta; trainer, Johnny Devereaux; and Tommy Daly who did great work for amateur boxing by bringing top-class fighters to Cork.

We said our goodbyes by the gates of his Alma Mater, the North Monastery, and I watched as he strode out the boreen like a man half his age. It is the opinion of many good judges that if Séamus Cummins had not turned professional he would have been one of the greatest amateur boxers of all time. We shall never know.

Katty Barry's
Cork's first nightclub

Recently, while strolling along Cornmarket St - better known as the Coal Quay Market - my mind wandered back to when I was a small garsún. My mother, with me tagging along like an obedient puppy, was a regular visitor to this famous, open-air market. To me it was the pounding heartbeat of the city. How times have changed. Memories came flooding back: the unique voices of the wrinkle-faced traders; those timeless women, the salt of the earth, wrapped in their black shawls as they higgled and haggled in various forms of colourful Corkese inveigling customers to buy anything from a double bed to bunch of bananas: the sing-song come-all-

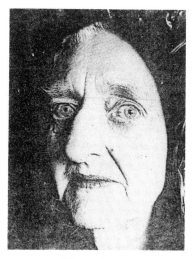

Katty Barry
COURTESY EXAMINER

ye's, often accompanied by a banjo or fiddle, wafting through the windows of the numerous pubs, most of them early morning houses ready and willing to facilitate the rural, thirsty traders. Add to this the contrasting smells and noisy excitement of the nervous animals: restless horses and donkeys, barking dogs and fluttering ducks, geese and chickens. This whole scenario was like an Aladdin's cave for an impressionable boy like me. I loved it when one of the kind old ladies gave me a maternal wink and slipped me an apple, or an orange, behind my mother's back. It was our little secret. The old place-names, which were so descriptive, have always fascinated me: Potato Quay, Cockpit Lane and Timber Quay.

The Coal Quay also had a certain fame because Katty Barry, a legend in her own lifetime, lived there. She was an intelligent, strong-willed woman who ran her establishment with a fist of female iron. It was Cork's first nightclub. In reality, it was a small late-night shebeen, with sawdust on the floor, which provided crubeens and illicit alcohol for the eager customers. Everybody was catered for; there was no class

Cornmarket Street
COURTESY HARRIET SHEEHY

distinction. She was one of Cork's great characters and, sadly, after a long, colourful innings, she died in 1982.

The modern Coal Quay is but a pale shadow of it's former self. There are several reasons for this: gradually, the dealers' houses were demolished and they moved out to the edge of the city. And, as time passed, they found it more and more difficult to get in and out to their stalls. These stalls were once handed down, and proudly accepted, from generation to generation, but shawls are now long gone and young people are slow to stand out in the open eight hours a day for very little reward. Another reason is the advent of supermarkets. There are now a plethora of supermarkets in the outskirts of the city, and it is more practical for people to shop locally and avoid the hustle and bustle of the city centre. The pulse of the Coal Quay may have slowed down but its heart will live forever.

Women of the Coal Quay.
COURTESY EXAMINER

Bunny O'Hare
Have Bell - Will Travel

Bunny O'Hare, timekeeper supreme, is 86 years young. He is probably the most respected figure in Irish boxing. It is a common sight to see him ringside anywhere in Ireland, clutching his beloved bell and keeping one eye on a stopwatch and the other on the fight. And he is also a familiar figure in the blackness of night barely making it back to his local after officiating in some remote corner of the country. You can't miss him; he usually has a bag of boxing gloves under one arm and his beloved bell under the other.

"Boxing is in my blood," he says. "If I gave it up I wouldn't last another day." Educated at the Eason's Hill academy, he is an avid sports fan: he was deeply interested in draghunting, played soccer with Rockville, but boxing took up a major part of his young life.

Born and reared in Fair Lane, Bunny has seen huge social changes in the Northside. He fondly recalls the playground of his youth: Trimbath's Lane, Mannixes Arch, Step Lane, Bailey's Lane and Dead Man's Lane.

"That was long before the emergence of Gurranebraher," he reminded me. His family is like a who's who in boxing: "My uncle, Jerry Blake, was the British Army lightweight champion; the brother, Tucker, boxed with Sunnyside; my nephew, Terry St Ledger, turned pro for a while. In fact, four generation of us boxed: myself; my son, Séamus; Séamus' son, Martin; and his son, Richard."

As we relaxed in his cosy front room, surrounded by trophies and boxing books on the likes of Jack Johnson, Jim Corbett and the great Sugar Ray Robinson, I asked him who was the best he had seen. He paused for a while.

"It's very hard to say," he replied. "Paddy Martin was outstanding. There was Séamus Cummins, Ray Donnelly, Séanie O'Mahony, Connie Morrissey, Neilly Dunne was good, Willy O'Leary, Timmy McNamee, Don Murray, Paul Power was a fine boxer and coach. I could go on all night but if I had to pick one it would be Tommy Hyde. Tommy was special. Of course, I'm proud of my own club, Father Horgan's. We were the first club to bring the Juvenile Cup out of Dublin. We had a string of fine young boxers including three who each won three Irish titles: Connie Buckley, Dave Dulea and Michael Aherne."

Then this sprightly octogenarian took out his diary and, with a twinkle in his blue eyes, skimmed through it.

"One of the highlights was doing an Irish selection against the US, and a few months ago I did Ireland and France in Waterford. Just before Christmas I had 80 fights in one week. January 15th there was 18 in Cobh, January 22nd I had 20 fights, the next night another 20 in Millstreet."

By the time he reached February I was exhausted just from listening to him. He told me that he was going to retire 20 years ago but the county board wouldn't let him. One fact sums up this incredible man: the year before last he was the timekeeper for all the 191 fights decided in the National Stadium in Dublin. Bunny O'Hare is a charming gentleman and has a zest for life which puts us all to shame. Before I left I asked him if he ever considered retirement.

"Retirement?" he laughed, "the best is yet to come, boy."

Two Cork Stalwarts – Bunny and Jack Lynch.

Roger Tuohy
Little Hercules

Roger Tuohy has had hurling in his blood since the day he was born. He may be a small man but he has a huge heart. That great commentator, Michael O'Hehir, christened him "Little Hercules." Roger has clear memories of his childhood. "I was always very acrobatic," he recalls. "As a young boy I often walked all the way to school on my hands. We lived near Farrenferris Seminary in Farranree. I used to climb over the high wall and search for discarded, broken hurleys. I could only use half a hurley then because a whole hurley was bigger than myself. We played on the road every day. There was hardly any traffic then. Although I played regularly with the North Mon I was introduced to Na Piarsaigh club at eight years of age and so began a life-long association with the club."

His first taste of success was with the school. As he was captain he had to sit out in front for the team photograph. A pair of boots had to be borrowed for the occasion. "They nearly killed my poor feet," he remembers. Now and then he also found and wore odd stockings and boots which were several sizes too big for him.

But Roger always felt more comfortable wearing rubber dollies, even in muddy conditions. He wore them right up to senior hurling. He made his senior debut when he was just 14 years old. "Hurling was much tougher then. In one match against the Barr's I got my teeth knocked out and I lay on the ground feeling sorry for myself. A mentor shouted, 'get up quick and forget your good looks.' At that time conditions were very poor. Teams togged off at the side of a field. If it rained your clothes got soaked. The first dressing-room I ever used was up in Delaney's pitch. It was a railway carriage full of cows. The cows had to be hunted out to let us in, but it was magic. The first shower we ever had was at a country match. We togged off in a farmyard and used a tap on the wall to wash. It was heaven. And after-match celebrations were simpler then. If we won anything Tony Hegarty brought us all down to An Stad in Blackpool and treated us to milk and cakes."

Like most young boys, Christy Ring was Roger's idol. They first met in the dressing-room as he had just finished playing for Cork minors and Christy was preparing for a senior game. They played against each other a few years later in a heated Na Piarsaigh versus Glen Rovers encounter.

Cork Minor Team 1961 – A 16 year old Roger sitting front left.

Roger has mixed feelings about that match. "I was playing very well until I got a belt of a hurley in the ankle. As I was being carried off in agony I learned that Christy was the culprit, and I actually felt honoured." They went on to become great personal friends. Every Monday night Christy called up to Farranree for a cup of tea and a passionate discussion about hurling.

Once, as a teenager, Roger got a little disillusioned with his lot and ran away with a circus. For six weeks he toured Ireland working as a clown and an acrobat. Twice a night, as part of his act, he used to summersault on to a passing horse. "Although I loved it it was tough going: living in a caravan, long hours, often seven days a week, it was a continuous cycle of work. We were just leaving for Scotland when my father tracked me down and begged me to return home. Na Piarsaigh were playing in the county final and were looking for my assistance."

Roger marching with the Cork team followed by Tomás Ryan, Gerald and Justin McCarthy against Tipp in the Munster Final 1969.

In 1965 he graduated to the Cork senior team but after a row with offialdom he didn't play for two years.By now he had turned to squash and athletics winning a sackful of trophies for sprinting. He also jumped six feet to win a high jump competion but was disqualified because his method of jumping was deemed to be illegal.

From 1967 to 1970 he was a regular on the Cork senior hurling team. The year 1969 was full of ups and downs. Cork won the league, the Oireachtas Cup and the Munster Championship but then lost the All-Ireland to Kilkenny. Cork were seven points up just before half-time yet Kilkenny completely outplayed them against the wind in the second half. Roger was substituted just after the interval. "It was the biggest disappointment in my life," he recalls. "I felt I could have been switched on to Frank Cummins who was running riot, but that's sport. Gerald McCarthy, who now trains Waterford, was on that team. He was the best player I ever played with and also the best player I ever played against. Cork won the All-Ireland on the following year but I missed out because I was injured in a car crash."

By now he was a household name. His habit of doing a summersault with his hurley as he ran onto the pitch was picked up by an RTE camera and, for months, this was used to introduce Saturday sport on TV.

Then, out of the blue, there was a knock on his door and he was invited to join the army. He signed on at 4 o'clock, was sworn in, and played in a final that evening. "I went up a civilian and came down a soldier." he laughed. Twelve months later there was another final but he was out of action and in plaster-of-Paris from his waist to his neck. But the army, with true military determination, removed the plaster. Roger played, the match was won, and he was immediately replastered.

Life had other plans for Roger: he was bitten by the showbiz bug and toured Munster as a gymnast in a variety show with Tony Hegarty. One night they arrived very early to do their act in a well-known hotel. To pass the time away they made the mistake of having a few drinks. Two hours later, the worse for wear, they struggled through their routine. The finale consisted of Tony lying crucifix-like flat on his back before dramatically lifting his partner straight up at arm's length. But the alcohol had taken its effect. A ferocious breaking of wind was heard. Roger collapsed on Tony, his knee colliding with his groin. The audience collapsed in tears of laughter. They thought it was part of the act. The embarrassed duo made a hasty retreat. They didn't even collect their fee. Roger saw the light and retired from show business, then had five eventful years as a city bar-owner before settling down as a painting contractor.

"At least I have one unusual record," he said. "At five feet two and a half inches I'm the smallest hurler ever to play in an All-Ireland final."

He is proud of the fact that his three sons also wore the red jersey of Cork but his one sporting regret is that he never won a senior county medal. When he was playing, Na Piarsaigh were a much smaller club. Down through the years he was constantly poached by the big city clubs but refused to go. "I could never leave Na Piarsaigh," he said. "Sure they reared me."

Washbrew Lane

Washbrew Lane was a spindly, twisting, red-bricked lane which ran from the bottom of Fair Hill up to a dead end at Fahey's Well near Kingston's farm. When I recall this playground of my youth it conjures up a deluge of paradoxical memories: simplicity, happiness, uncertainty, poverty, whitewash, ignorance, religion, Jeyes fluid, beagles, bowlplayers, innocence, TB, polio, fleas and DDT. The lane was made up of 27 small houses, each one - with its own birdcage - more colourful than the next. It was an everyday cacophony of sound: dogs, cats, pigeons, goats, canaries, pigs and especially children; there seemed to be children everywhere, and it was a common sight to see a passionate confrontation between two mothers concerning their beloved offspring. Against all that, a genuine love and neighbourliness always prevailed. It was as if being poor was a common bond. Lady Poverty was a constant

Shaws Alley
COURTESY EXAMINER

75

One of the many lanes near the Norh Infirmary.
COURTESY WOLFHOUND PRESS

companion and she seldom lowered her ugly head. Everyone was equal as they scratched and struggled to stay above the breadline. There were no jobs or money and even less education. Yet it was a hugely exciting place to live - alive with tremendous characters: Pakey Holland, Josher Walsh and his son Ritchie Boy, Lizzie Maloney, Spud Murphy, Annie Doyle, Hada O'Callaghan and his son Guy, Porridge Lynch, Maggie Webb and Agoo Murphy. Agoo was the proud owner of the very first car any of us wide-eyed children had ever seen. We stood around in awe of this strange gleaming object as if it were something from outer space.

Although they were spartan times, humour and initiative were never very far away. One day Hada's two sons were fooling about in the front room when they accidently knocked, and broke, a vase from the mantlepiece. They heard their father coming and, quick as a flash, they placed the innocent cat on the mantlepiece. Hada put two and two together and took it out on the unfortunate cat. Hada was an ageless and extremely likeable rogue and was better known as the "bastern man" because he described everything in this way. If it wasn't the "bastern" weather it was the "bastern" government. There was an after-hours raid on his local one night. He dashed out to the yard and began to escape over a high wall. He called out to the man behind him to give him a leg-up. It was a young gard who had him caught by the leg. "Come down before you break your neck," the gard said, and left him off with a warning. Josher Walsh lived next door to Hada. For some weeks he was out of work and receiving welfare money. One day the social welfare lady was doing her rounds in the lane checking out people. Unfortunately, Josher was in the pub when he was supposed to be in bed. Panic set in. His wife, Annie, swung into action. Some men were playing cards nearby. She ran over and grabbed one, Cal Murphy, who was particularly pale-faced and half Josher's size, and dragged him protesting to the bedroom to act as a substitute husband. Moments later, the welfare lady entered the Walsh home and gazed sympathetically at the fearful Cal as he lay in bed with the blanket tucked up under his chin to conceal his clothes. She took one look at him and said, "Oh, my God, you look terrible, Josher. Stay in bed for a week."

When I was about ten years of age I had to call to a number of houses every day with a donkey and cart and collect waste food to feed the pigs. One day, when I left my last port of call - a house at the bottom of Fair Hill - I discovered that the donkey had disappeared. I was mystified. I knew that he couldn't have made it up the steep hill and he was nowhere

Off Paul Street – Note Bird Cages
COURTESY EXAMINER

78

to be seen anywhere in the lane. The only people around were a man and woman berthed in a dark corner. They were in the throws of passion. Undaunted, I walked over, tapped the man on the shoulder and naively said, "Excuse me, sir, but you didn't happen to see a donkey and cart passing up along?" I thought it was a perfectly reasonable question at the time, but it may have spoiled the moment because his reply is unrepeatable. The term coitus interruptus springs to mind. The donkey, like any sensible animal, was patiently waiting for me when I got home.

At the top of the lane there were the remains of a dancehall, and a boxing club which eventually blew down one stormy night. This area was where it all happened. We played "kick the can," "spin the carrot"; we couldn't afford a bottle, and "kiss or torture". Being a natural coward I couldn't face any form of torture, so I kissed my first girl behind that club. I'll never forget that kiss. It was all saliva and vinegar. She was eating a bag of chips at the time.

Just up from the club was a rundown old well called Fahey's Well. For me, two vivid memories sum up the fifties: one was that, every year, buckets of water were taken from the well and the local women used to religiously scrub down every inch of the lane for the feast of Corpus Cristi; and, secondly, a girl got married one day; she borrowed a ring from Celia Hurley in the corner shop and walked down to the North Cathedral for the ceremony, with a flock of inquisitive children trailing in her wake. She got married, walked back up, returned the ring to her friend and had a knees-up in her little house. They were such practical times.

Opposite the well, a mangle field stood in splendid isolation. It was a bumpy, barren patch covered with nettles but, to us, it was heaven. Every game whether it was hurling, rugby or soccer was fought out with fierce passion. Past the top of the lane there was an area called Bonties. It consisted of a narrow stream which was banked up with sods every summer. Everybody learned to swim here; there were dozens of potato plots which were let out to local families; and, finally, the place was teeming with horses. Owners put their horses out to graze here every night, so all the boys were in the enviable position of playing cowboys on real horses.

There was a certain sadness when Washbrew Lane was demolished in the summer of 1956 to make way for the North Link Rd. For the last 43 years the back gardens of one side of the lane were still visible. I knew every one of those gardens so well - each sloping, craggy overgrown one of them was like an old friend. That's where we acted out our sporting dreams: throwing big rocks as if we were shotputting for Ireland; jumping over strings and wires in the high jump; scoring the winning goal in a cup final, always with a diving header. This was our field of dreams, our Croke Park, our Wembley, our Olympics. Alas, none of us ever really made it.

These old gardens were like relics or headstones - daily reminders of a time long gone. Recently they were removed and this very area was beautifully landscaped. Washbrew Lane is now a distant memory overflowing with laughter, tripe and drisheen, shawls, half-doors and unfulfilled dreams.